TEACHINGS
OF JESUS

TEACHINGS OF JESUS

THE SERMON ON THE MOUNT
AND PARABLES OF THE
NEW TESTAMENT

THE HOLY BIBLE
KING JAMES VERSION

penguin books

PENGUIN BOOKS
Published by the Penguin Group
Penguin Books USA Inc., 375 Hudson Street,
New York, New York 10014, U.S.A.
Penguin Books Ltd, 27 Wrights Lane,
London W8 5TZ, England
Penguin Books Australia Ltd, Ringwood,
Victoria, Australia
Penguin Books Canada Ltd, 10 Alcorn Avenue,
Toronto, Ontario, Canada M4V 3B2
Penguin Books (N.Z.) Ltd, 182–190 Wairau Road,
Auckland 10, New Zealand

Penguin Books Ltd, Registered Offices:
Harmondsworth, Middlesex, England

Published in Penguin Books 1995

ISBN 0 14 60.0088 9

Printed in the United States of America

CONTENTS

The Sermon on the Mount
(From the Gospel of Matthew)

And seeing the multitudes, he went up into a mountain: and when he was set, his disciples came unto him: And he opened his mouth, and taught them, saying,

Blessed *are* the poor in spirit: for their's is the kingdom of heaven. Blessed *are* they that mourn: for they shall be comforted. Blessed *are* the meek: for they shall inherit the earth. Blessed *are* they which do hunger and thirst after righteousness: for they shall be filled. Blessed *are* the merciful: for they shall obtain mercy. Blessed *are* the pure in heart: for they shall see God. Blessed *are* the peacemakers: for they shall be called the children of God. Blessed *are* they which are persecuted for righteousness' sake: for their's is the kingdom of heaven. Blessed are ye, when *men* shall revile you, and persecute *you*, and shall say all manner of evil against you falsely, for my sake. Rejoice, and be exceeding glad: for great *is* your reward in heaven: for so persecuted they the prophets which were before you.

Ye are the salt of the earth: but if the salt have lost his

savour, wherewith shall it be salted? it is thenceforth good for nothing, but to be cast out, and to be trodden under foot of men. Ye are the light of the world. A city that is set on an hill cannot be hid. Neither do men light a candle, and put it under a bushel, but on a candlestick; and it giveth light unto all that are in the house. Let your light so shine before men, that they may see your good works, and glorify your Father, which is in heaven.

Think not that I am come to destroy the law, or the prophets: I am not come to destroy, but to fulfil. For verily I say unto you, Till heaven and earth pass, one jot or one tittle shall in no wise pass from the law, till all be fulfilled. Whosoever therefore shall break one of these least commandments, and shall teach men so, he shall be called the least in the kingdom of heaven: but whosoever shall do and teach *them*, the same shall be called great in the kingdom of heaven. For I say unto you, That except your righteousness shall exceed *the righteousness* of the scribes and Pharisees, ye shall in no case enter into the kingdom of heaven.

Ye have heard that it was said by them of old time, Thou shalt not kill; and whosoever shall kill shall be in danger of the judgment: But I say unto you, That whosoever is angry with his brother without a cause shall be in danger of the judgment: and whosoever shall say to his brother, Raca, shall be in danger of the council: but whosoever shall say, Thou fool, shall be in danger of hell fire. Therefore if thou bring thy gift to the altar, and there rememberest that thy brother hath ought against thee; Leave there thy gift before the altar, and go thy way; first be reconciled to thy brother, and then come and offer thy gift. Agree with thine adversary quickly, whiles thou art in the way with him; lest at any time the adversary deliver thee to the judge, and the judge deliver thee to the officer, and thou be cast into prison. Verily I say unto thee, Thou shalt by no means come out thence, till thou hast paid the uttermost farthing.

Ye have heard that it was said by them of old time, Thou shalt not commit adultery: But I say unto you, That whosoever looketh on a woman to lust after her hath committed adultery with her already in his heart. And if thy right eye offend thee, pluck it out, and cast *it* from thee: for it is profitable for thee that one of thy members should perish, and not *that* thy whole body should be cast into hell. And if thy right hand offend thee, cut it off, and cast *it* from thee: for it is profitable for thee that one of thy members should perish, and not *that* thy whole body should be cast into hell. It hath been said, Whosoever shall put away his wife, let him give her a writing of divorcement: But I say unto you, That whosoever shall put away his wife, saving for the cause of fornication, causeth her to commit adultery: and whosoever shall marry her that is divorced committeth adultery.

Again, ye have heard that it hath been said by them of old time, Thou shalt not forswear thyself, but shalt perform unto the Lord thine oaths: But I say unto you, Swear not at all; neither by heaven; for it is God's throne: Nor by the earth; for it is his footstool: neither Jerusalem; for it is the city of the great King. Neither shalt thou swear by thy head, because thou canst not make one hair white or black. But let your communication be, Yea, yea; Nay, nay: for whatsoever is more than these cometh of evil.

Ye have heard that it hath been said, An eye for an eye, and a tooth for a tooth: But I say unto you, That ye resist not evil: but whosoever shall smite thee on thy right cheek, turn to him the other also. And if any man will sue thee at the law, and take away thy coat, let him have *thy* cloke also. And whosoever shall compel thee to go a mile, go with him twain. Give to him that asketh thee, and from him that would borrow of thee turn not thou away.

Ye have heard that it hath been said, Thou shalt love thy neighbour, and hate thine enemy. But I say unto you, Love your enemies, bless them that curse you, do good to them that hate you, and pray for them which despitefully use you, and persecute you; That ye may be the children of your Father which is in heaven: for he maketh his sun to rise on the evil and on the good, and sendeth rain on the just and on the unjust. For if ye love them which love you, what reward have ye? do not even the publicans the same? And if ye salute your brethren only, what do ye more *than others?* do not even the publicans so? Be ye therefore perfect, even as your Father which is in heaven is perfect.

Take heed that ye do not your alms before men, to be seen of them: otherwise ye have no reward of your Father which is in heaven. Therefore when thou doest *thine* alms, do not sound a trumpet before thee, as the hypocrites do in the synagogues and in the streets, that they may have glory of men. Verily I say unto you, They have their reward. But when thou doest alms, let not thy left hand know what thy right hand doeth: That thine alms may be in secret: and thy Father which seeth in secret himself shall reward thee openly.

And when thou prayest, thou shalt not be as the hypocrites *are:* for they love to pray standing in the synagogues and in the corners of the streets, that they may be seen of men. Verily I say unto you, They have their reward. But thou, when thou prayest, enter into thy closet, and when thou hast shut thy door, pray to thy Father which is in secret; and thy Father which seeth in secret shall reward thee openly. But when ye pray, use not vain repetitions, as the heathen *do:* for they think that they shall be heard for their much speaking. Be not ye therefore like unto them: for your Father knoweth what things ye have need of, before ye ask him. After this manner therefore pray ye: Our Father which art in heaven, Hallowed be thy name. Thy kingdom come. Thy will be done in earth, as *it is* in heaven. Give us this day our daily bread. And forgive us our debts, as we forgive our debtors. And lead us not into temptation, but deliver us from evil: For thine is the kingdom, and the power, and the glory, for ever. Amen. For if ye forgive men their trespasses, your heavenly Father will also forgive you: But if ye forgive not men their trespasses, neither will your Father forgive your trespasses.

Moreover when ye fast, be not, as the hypocrites, of a sad countenance: for they disfigure their faces, that they may appear unto men to fast. Verily I say unto you, They have their reward. But thou, when thou fastest, anoint thine head, and wash thy face; That thou appear not unto men to fast; but unto thy Father which is in secret: and thy Father, which seeth in secret, shall reward thee openly.

Lay not up for yourselves treasures upon earth, where moth and rust doth corrupt, and where thieves break through and steal: But lay up for yourselves treasures in heaven, where neither moth nor rust doth corrupt, and where thieves do not break through nor steal: For where your treasure is, there will your heart be also. The light of the body is the eye: if therefore thine eye be single, thy whole body shall be full of light. But if thine eye be evil, thy whole body shall be full of darkness. If therefore the light that is in thee be darkness, how great *is* that darkness!

No man can serve two masters: for either he will hate the one, and love the other; or else he will hold to the one, and despise the other. Ye cannot serve God and mammon. Therefore I say unto you, Take no thought for your life, what ye shall eat, or what ye shall drink; nor yet for your body, what ye shall put on. Is not the life more than meat, and the body than raiment? Behold the fowls of the air: for they sow not, neither do they reap, nor gather into barns; yet your heavenly Father feedeth them. Are ye not much better than they? Which of you by taking thought can add one cubit unto his stature? And why take ye thought for raiment? Consider the lilies of the field, how they grow; they toil not, neither do they spin: And yet I say unto you, That even Solomon in all his glory was not arrayed like one of these. Wherefore, if God so clothe the grass of the field, which to day is, and to morrow is cast into the oven, *shall he* not much more *clothe* you, O ye of little faith? Therefore take no thought, saying, What shall we eat? or, What shall we drink? or, Wherewithal shall we be clothed? (For after all these things do the Gentiles seek:) for your heavenly Father knoweth that ye have need of all these things. But seek ye first the kingdom of God, and his righteousness; and all these things shall be added unto you. Take therefore no thought for the morrow: for the morrow shall take thought for the things of itself. Sufficient unto the day *is* the evil thereof.

Judge not, that ye be not judged. For with what judgment ye judge, ye shall be judged: and with what measure ye mete, it shall be measured to you again. And why beholdest thou the mote that is in thy brother's eye, but considerest not the beam that is in thine own eye? Or how wilt thou say to thy brother, Let me pull out the mote out of thine eye; and, behold, a beam *is* in thine own eye? Thou hypocrite, first cast out the beam out of thine own eye; and then shalt thou see clearly to cast out the mote out of thy brother's eye.

Give not that which is holy unto the dogs, neither cast

ye your pearls before swine, neither cast ye your pearls before swine, lest they trample them under their feet, and turn again and rend you.

Ask, and it shall be given you; seek, and ye shall find; knock, and it shall be opened unto you: For every one that asketh receiveth; and he that seeketh findeth; and to him that knocketh it shall be opened. Or what man is there of you, whom if his son ask bread, will he give him a stone? Or if he ask a fish, will he give him a serpent? If ye then, being evil, know how to give good gifts unto your children, how much more shall your Father which is in heaven give good things to them that ask him? Therefore all things whatsoever ye would that men should do to you, do ye even so to them: for this is the law and the prophets.

Enter ye in at the strait gate: for wide *is* the gate, and broad *is* the way, that leadeth to destruction, and many there be which go in thereat: Because strait *is* the gate, and narrow *is* the way, which leadeth unto life, and few there be that find it.

Beware of false prophets, which come to you in sheep's clothing, but inwardly they are ravening wolves. Ye shall know them by their fruits. Do men gather grapes of thorns, or figs of thistles? Even so every good tree bringeth forth good fruit; but a corrupt tree bringeth forth evil fruit. A good tree cannot bring forth evil fruit, neither *can* a corrupt tree bring forth good fruit. Every tree that bringeth not forth good fruit is hewn down, and cast into the fire. Wherefore by their fruits ye shall know them.

Not every one that saith unto me, Lord, Lord, shall enter into the kingdom of heaven; but he that doeth the will of my Father which is in heaven. Many will say to me in that day, Lord, Lord, have we not prophesied in thy name? and in thy name have cast out devils? and in thy name done many wonderful works? And then will I profess unto them, I never knew you: depart from me, ye that work iniquity.

Therefore whosoever heareth these sayings of mine, and doeth them, I will liken him unto a wise man, which built his house upon a rock: And the rain descended, and the floods came, and the winds blew, and beat upon that house; and it fell not: for it was founded upon a rock. And every one that heareth these sayings of mine, and doeth them not, shall be likened unto a foolish man, which built his house upon the sand: And the rain descended, and the floods came, and the winds blew, and beat upon that house; and it fell: and great was the fall of it.

And it came to pass, when Jesus had ended these sayings, the people were astonished at his doctrine: For he taught them as one having authority, and not as the scribes.

The Parables of the Sower, the Mustard Seed,
the Tares, and the Hidden Treasure
(From the Gospel of Matthew)

And he spake many things unto them in parables, saying, Behold, a sower went forth to sow: And when he sowed, some *seeds* fell by the way side, and the fowls came and devoured them up: Some fell upon stony places, where they had not much earth: and forthwith they sprung up, because they had no deepness of earth: And when the sun was up, they were scorched; and because they had no root, they withered away. And some fell among thorns; and the thorns sprung up, and choked them: But other fell into good ground, and brought forth fruit, some an hundredfold, some sixtyfold, some thirtyfold. Who hath ears to hear, let him hear.

And the disciples came, and said unto him, Why speakest thou unto them in parables?

He answered and said unto them, Because it is given unto you to know the mysteries of the kingdom of heaven, but to them it is not given. For whosoever hath, to him shall be given, and he shall have more abundance: but whosoever hath not, from him shall be taken away even that he hath. Therefore speak I to them in parables: because they seeing see not; and hearing they hear not, neither do they understand. And in them is fulfilled the prophecy of Esaisas, which saith, By hearing ye shall hear, and shall not understand; and seeing ye shall see, and shall not perceive: For this people's heart is waxed gross, and *their* ears are dull of hearing, and their eyes they have closed; lest at any time they should see with *their* eyes, and hear with *their* ears, and should understand with *their* heart, and should be converted, and I should heal them. But blessed *are* your eyes, for they see: and your ears, for they hear. For verily I say unto you, That many prophets and righteous *men* have desired to see *those things* which ye see, and have not seen *them;* and to hear *those things* which ye hear, and have not heard *them.*

Hear ye therefore the parable of the sower. When any one heareth the word of the kingdom, and understandeth *it* not, then cometh the wicked *one*, and catcheth away that which was sown in his heart. This is he which received seed by the way side. But he that received the seed into stony places, the same is he that heareth the word, and anon with joy receiveth it; Yet hath he not root in himself, but dureth for a while: for when tribulation or persecution ariseth because of the word, by and by he is offended. He also that received seed among the thorns is he that heareth the word; and the care of this world, and the deceitfulness of riches, choke the word, and he becometh unfruitful. But he that received seed into the good ground is he that heareth the word, and understandeth *it;* which also beareth fruit, and bringeth forth, some an hundredfold, some sixty, some thirty.

Another parable put he forth unto them, saying, The kingdom of heaven is likened unto a man which sowed good seed in his field: But while men slept, his enemy came and sowed tares among the wheat, and went his way. But when the blade was sprung up, and brought forth fruit, then appeared the tares also. So the servants of the householder came and said unto him, Sir, didst not thou sow good seed in thy field? from whence then hath it tares? He said unto them, An enemy hath done this. The servants said unto him, Wilt thou then that we go and gather them up? But he said, Nay; lest while ye gather up the tares, ye root up also the wheat with them. Let both grow together until the harvest: and in the time of harvest I will say to the reapers, Gather ye together first the tares, and bind them in bundles to burn them: but gather the wheat into my barn.

Another parable put he forth unto them, saying, The kingdom of heaven is like to a grain of mustard seed, which a man took, and sowed in his field: Which indeed is the least of all seeds: but when it is grown, it is the greatest among herbs, and becometh a tree, so that the birds of the air come and lodge in the branches thereof.

Another parable spake he unto them; The kingdom of heaven is like unto leaven, which a woman took, and hid in three measures of meal, till the whole was leavened.

All these things spake Jesus unto the multitude in parables; and without a parable spake he not unto them: That it might be fulfilled which was spoken by the prophet, saying, I will open my mouth in parables; I will utter things which have been kept secret from the foundation of the world. Then Jesus sent the multitude away, and went into the house: and his disciples came unto him, saying, Declare unto us the parable of the tares of the field.

He answered and said unto them, He that soweth the good seed is the Son of man; The field is the world; the good seed are the children of the kingdom; but the tares are the children of the wicked *one;* The enemy that sowed them is the devil; the harvest is the end of the world; and the reapers are the angels. As therefore the tares are gathered and burned in the fire; so shall it be in the end of this world. The Son of man shall send forth his angels, and they shall gather out of his kingdom all things that offend, and them which do iniquity; And shall cast them into a furnace of fire: there shall be wailing and gnashing of teeth. Then shall the righteous shine forth as the sun in the kingdom of their Father. Who hath ears to hear, let him hear.

Again, the kingdom of heaven is like unto treasure hid in a field; the which when a man hath found, he hideth, and for joy thereof goeth and selleth all that he hath, and buyeth that field.

Again, the kingdom of heaven is like unto a merchant man, seeking goodly pearls: Who, when he had found one pearl of great price, went and sold all that he had, and bought it.

Again, the kingdom of heaven is like unto a net, that was cast into the sea, and gathered of every kind: Which, when it was full, they drew to shore, and sat down, and gathered the good into vessels, but cast the bad away. So shall it be at the end of the world: the angels shall come forth, and sever the wicked from among the just, And shall cast them into the furnace of fire: there shall be wailing and gnashing of teeth.

Jesus saith unto them, Have ye understood all these things? *They say unto him, Yea, Lord.*

Then said he unto them, Therefore every scribe *which is* instructed unto the kingdom of heaven is like unto a man *that is* an householder, which bringeth forth out of his treasure *things* new and old.

And it came to pass, that *when Jesus had finished these parables, he departed thence.*

The Parable of the Labourers in the Vineyard
(From the Gospel of Matthew)

For the kingdom of heaven is like unto a man *that is* an householder, which went out early in the morning to hire labourers into his vineyard. And when he had agreed with the labourers for a penny a day, he sent them into his vineyard. And he went out about the third hour, and saw others standing idle in the marketplace. And said unto them; Go ye also into the vineyard, and whatsoever is right I will give you. And they went their way. Again he went out about the sixth and ninth hour, and did likewise. And about the eleventh hour he went out, and found others standing idle, and saith unto them, Why stand ye here all the day idle? They say unto him, Because no man hath hired us. He saith unto them, Go ye also into the vineyard; and whatsoever is right, *that* shall ye receive. So when even was come, the lord of the vineyard saith unto his steward, Call the labourers, and give them *their* hire, beginning from the last unto the first. And when they came that *were hired* about the eleventh hour, they received every man a penny. But when the first came, they supposed that they should have received more; and they likewise received every man a penny. And when they had received *it*, they murmured against the goodman of the house, Saying, These last have wrought *but* one hour, and thou hast made them equal unto us, which have borne the burden and heat of the day. But he answered one of them, and said, Friend, I do thee no wrong: didst not thou agree with me for a penny? Take *that* thine *is*, and go thy way: I will give unto this last, even as unto thee. Is it not lawful for me to do what I will with mine own? Is thine eye evil, because I am good? So the last shall be first, and the first last: for many be called, but few chosen.

The Parables of the Father and His Two Sons
and of the Householder and the Husbandmen
(From the Gospel of Matthew)

But what think ye? A *certain* man had two sons; and he came to the first, and said, Son, go work to day in my vineyard. He answered and said, I will not: but afterward he repented, and went. And he came to the second, and said likewise. And he answered and said, I *go*, sir: and went not. Whether of them twain did the will of *his* father? *They say unto him, The first. Jesus saith unto them,* Verily I say unto you, That the publicans and the harlots go into the kingdom of God before you. For John came unto you in the way of righteousness, and ye believed him not: but the publicans and the harlots believed him: and ye, when ye had seen *it*, repented not afterward, that ye might believe him.

Hear another parable: There was a certain householder, which planted a vineyard, and hedged it round about, and digged a winepress in it, and built a tower, and let it out to husbandmen, and went into a far country: And when the time of the fruit drew near, he sent his servants to the husbandmen, that they might receive the fruits of it. And the husbandmen took his servants, and beat one, and killed another, and stoned another. Again, he sent other servants more than the first: and they did unto them likewise. But last of all he sent unto them his son, saying, They will reverence my son. But when the husbandmen saw the son, they said among themselves, This is the heir; come, let us kill him, and let us seize on his inheritance. And they caught him, and cast *him* out of the vineyard, and slew *him*. When the lord therefore of the vineyard cometh, what will he do unto those husbandmen?

They say unto him, He will miserably destroy those wicked men, and will let out his *vineyard unto other husbandmen, which shall render him the fruits in their seasons.*

Jesus saith unto them, Did ye never read in the scriptures, The stone which the builders rejected, the same is become the head of the corner: this is the Lord's doing, and it is marvellous in our eyes? Therefore say I unto you, The kingdom of God shall be taken from you, and given to a nation bringing forth the fruits thereof. And whosoever shall fall on this stone shall be broken: but on whomsoever it shall fall, it will grind him to powder.

The Parable of the Marriage of the King's Son
(From the Gospel of Matthew)

And Jesus answered and spake unto them again by parables, and said, The kingdom of heaven is like unto a certain king, which made a marriage for his son, And sent forth his servants to call them that were bidden to the wedding: and they would not come. Again, he sent forth other servants, saying, Tell them which are bidden, Behold, I have prepared my dinner: my oxen and *my* fatlings *are* killed, and all things *are* ready: come unto the marriage. But they made light of *it*, and went their ways, one to his farm, another to his merchandise: And the remnant took his servants, and entreated *them* spitefully, and slew *them*. But when the king heard *thereof*, he was wroth: and he sent forth his armies, and destroyed those murderers, and burned up their city. Then saith he to his servants, The wedding is ready, but they which were bidden were not worthy. Go ye therefore into the highways, and as many as ye shall find, bid to the marriage. So those servants went out into the highways, and gathered together all as many as they found, both bad and good: and the wedding was furnished with guests.

And when the king came in to see the guests, he saw there a man which had not on a wedding garment: And he saith unto him, Friend, how camest thou in hither not having a wedding garment? And he was speechless. Then said the king to the servants, Bind him hand and foot, and take him away, and cast *him* into outer darkness; there shall be weeping and gnashing of teeth. For many are called, but few *are* chosen.

The Parable of the Fig Tree
(From the Gospel of Matthew)

Now learn a parable of the fig tree; When his branch is yet tender, and putteth forth leaves, ye know that summer *is* nigh: So likewise ye, when ye shall see all these things, know that it is near, *even* at the doors. Verily I say unto you, This generation shall not pass, till all these things be fulfilled. Heaven and earth shall pass away, but my words shall not pass away.

The Parables of the Virgins, the Talents,
and the Sheep and the Goats
(From the Gospel of Matthew)

Then shall the kingdom of heaven be likened unto ten virgins, which took their lamps, and went forth to meet the bridegroom. And five of them were wise, and five *were* foolish. They that *were* foolish took their lamps, and took no oil with them: But the wise took oil in their vessels with their lamps. While the bridegroom tarried, they all slumbered and slept. And at midnight there was a cry made, Behold, the bridegroom cometh; go ye out to meet him. Then all those virgins arose, and trimmed their lamps. And the foolish said unto the wise, Give us of your oil; for our lamps are gone out. But the wise answered, saying, *Not so;* lest there be not enough for us and you: but go ye rather to them that sell, and buy for yourselves. And while they went to buy, the bridegroom came; and they that were ready went in with him to the marriage: and the door was shut. Afterward came also the other virgins, saying, Lord, Lord, open to us. But he answered and said, Verily I say unto you, I know you not.

Watch therefore, for ye know neither the day nor the hour wherein the Son of man cometh.

For *the kingdom of heaven is* as a man travelling into a far country, *who* called his own servants, and delivered unto them his goods. And unto one he gave five talents, to another two, and to another one; to every man according to his several ability; and straightway took his journey. Then he that had received the five talents went and traded with the same, and made *them* other five talents. And likewise he that *had received* two, he also gained other two. But he that had received one went and digged in the earth, and hid his lord's money. After a long time the lord of those servants cometh, and reckoneth with them. And so he that had received five talents came and brought other five talents, saying, Lord, thou deliveredst unto me five talents: behold, I have gained beside them five talents more. His lord said unto him, Well done, *thou* good and faithful servant: thou hast been faithful over a few things, I will make thee ruler over many things: enter thou into the joy of thy lord. He also that had received two talents came and said, Lord, thou deliveredst unto me two talents: behold, I have gained two other talents beside them. His lord said unto him, Well done, good and faithful servant; thou hast been faithful over a few things, I will make thee ruler over many things: enter thou into the joy of thy lord. Then he which had received the one talent came and said, Lord, I knew thee that thou art an hard man, reaping where thou hast not sown, and gathering where thou hast not strawed: And I was afraid, and went and hid thy talent in the earth: lo, *there* thou hast *that is* thine. His lord answered and said unto him, *Thou* wicked and slothful servant, thou knewest that I reap where I sowed not, and gather where I have not strawed: Thou oughtest therefore to have put my money to the exchangers, and *then* at my coming I should have received mine own with usury. Take therefore the talent from him, and give *it* unto him which hath ten talents. For unto every one that hath shall be given, and he shall have abundance: but from him that hath not shall be taken away even that which he hath, And cast ye the unprofitable servant into outer darkness: there shall be weeping and gnashing of teeth.

When the Son of man shall come in his glory, and all the holy angels with him, then shall he sit upon the throne of his glory: And before him shall be gathered all nations: and he shall separate them one from another, as a shepherd divideth *his* sheep from the goats: And he shall set the sheep on his right hand, but the goats on the left. Then shall the King say unto them on his right hand, Come, ye blessed of my Father, inherit the kingdom prepared for you from the foundation of the world: For I was an hungred, and ye gave me meat: I was thirsty, and ye gave me drink: I was a stranger, and ye took me in: Naked, and ye clothed me: I was sick, and ye visited me: I was in prison, and ye came unto me. Then shall the righteous answer him, saying, Lord, when saw we thee an hungred, and fed *thee?* or thirsty, and gave *thee* drink? When saw we thee a stranger, and took *thee* in? or naked, and clothed *thee?* Or when saw we thee sick, or in prison, and came unto thee? And the King shall answer and say unto them, Verily I say unto you, Inasmuch as ye have done *it* unto one of the least of these my brethren, ye have done *it* unto me. Then shall he say also unto them on the left hand, Depart from me, ye cursed, into everlasting fire, prepared for the devil and his angels: For I was an hungred, and ye gave me no meat: I was thirsty, and ye gave me no drink: I was a stranger, and ye took me not in: naked, and ye clothed me not: sick, and in prison, and ye visited me not. Then shall they also answer him, saying, Lord, when saw we thee an hungred, or athirst, or a stranger, or naked, or sick, or in prison, and did not minister unto thee? Then shall he answer them, saying, Verily I say unto you, Inasmuch as ye did *it* not to one of the least of these, ye did *it* not to me. And these shall go away into everlasting punishment: but the righteous into life eternal.

The Parable of the Two Debtors
(From the Gospel of Luke)

And one of the Pharisees desired him that he would eat with him. And he went into the Pharisee's house, and sat down to meat. And, behold, a woman in the city, which was a sinner, when she knew that Jesus sat at meat in the Pharisee's house, brought an alabaster box of ointment, And stood at his feet behind him weeping, and began to wash his feet with tears, and did wipe them with the hairs of her head, and kissed his feet, and anointed them with the ointment. Now when the Pharisee which had bidden him saw it, he spake within himself, saying, This man, if he were a prophet, would have known who and what manner of woman this is that toucheth him: for she is a sinner.

And Jesus answering said unto him, Simon I have somewhat to say unto thee. *And he saith, Master, say on.*

There was a certain creditor which had two debtors: the one owed five hundred pence, and the other fifty. And when they had nothing to pay, he frankly forgave them both. Tell me therefore, which of them will love him most?

Simon answered and said, I suppose that he, *to whom he forgave most. And he said unto him,* Thou hast rightly judged.

And he turned to the woman, and said unto Simon, Seest thou this woman? I entered into thine house, thou gavest me no water for my feet: but she hath washed my feet with tears, and wiped *them* with the hairs of her head. Thou gavest me no kiss: but this woman since the time I came in hath not ceased to kiss my feet. My head with oil thou didst not anoint: but this woman hath anointed my feet with ointment. Wherefore I say unto thee, Her sins, which are many, are forgiven; for she loved much: but to whom little is forgiven. *the same* loveth little. *And he said unto her,* Thy sins are forgiven.

And they that sat at meat with him began to say within themselves, Who is this that forgiveth sins also? And he said to the woman, Thy faith hath saved thee; go in peace.

The Parable of the Good Samaritan
(From the Gospel of Luke)

And, behold, a certain lawyer stood up, and tempted him, saying, Master, what shall I do to inherit eternal life?

He said unto him, What is written in the law? how readest thou?

And he answering said, Thou shalt love the Lord thy God with all thy heart, and with all thy soul, and with all they strength, and with all thy mind; and thy neighbour as thyself.

And he said unto him, Thou hast answered right: this do, and thou shalt live.

But he, willing to justify himself, said unto Jesus, And who is my neighbour?

And Jesus answering said, A certain *man* went down from Jerusalem to Jericho, and fell among thieves, which stripped him of his raiment, and wounded *him*, and departed, leaving *him* half dead. And by chance there came down a certain priest that way: and when he saw him, he passed by on the other side. And likewise a Levite, when he was at the place, came and looked *on him*, and passed by on the other side. But a certain Samaritan, as he journeyed, came where he was: and when he saw him, he had compassion *on him*, And went to *him*, and bound up his wounds, pouring in oil and wine, and set him on his own beast, and brought him to an inn, and took care of him. And on the morrow when he departed, he took out two pence, and gave *them* to the host, and said unto him, Take care of him; and whatsoever thou spendest more, when I come again, I will repay thee. Which now of these three, thinkest thou, was neighbour unto him that fell among the thieves?

And he said, He that shewed mercy on him. Then said Jesus unto him, Go, and do thou likewise.

The Parables of the Rich Fool and the
Servants Watching
(From the Gospel of Luke)

And he spake a parable unto them, saying, The ground of a certain rich man brought forth plentifully. And he thought within himself, saying, What shall I do, because I have no room where to bestow my fruits? And he said, This will I do: I will pull down my barns, and build greater; and there will I bestow all my fruits and my goods. And I will say to my soul, Soul, thou hast much goods laid up for many years; take thine ease, eat, drink, *and* be merry. But God said unto him, *Thou* fool, this night thy soul shall be required of thee: then whose shall those things be, which thou hast provided? So *is* he that layeth up treasure for himself, and is not rich toward God.

And he said unto his disciples, Therefore I say unto you, Take no thought for your life, what ye shall eat; neither for the body, what ye shall put on. The life is more than meat, and the body *is more* than raiment. Consider the ravens: for they neither sow nor reap; which neither have storehouse nor barn; and God feedeth them: how much more are ye better than the fowls? And which of you with taking thought can add to his stature one cubit? If ye then be not able to do that thing which is least, why take ye thought for the rest? Consider the lilies how they grow: they toil not, they spin not; and yet I say unto you, that Solomon in all his glory was not arrayed like one of these. If then God so clothe the grass, which is to day in the field, and to morrow is cast into the oven; how much more *will he clothe* you, O ye of little faith? And seek not ye what ye shall eat, or what ye shall drink, neither be ye of doubtful mind. For all these things do the nations of the world seek after: and your Father knoweth that ye have need of these things.

But rather seek ye the kingdom of God; and all these things shall be added unto you. Fear not, little flock; for it is your Father's good pleasure to give you the kingdom. Sell that ye have, and give alms; provide yourselves bags which wax not old, a treasure in the heavens that faileth not, where no thief approacheth, neither moth corrupteth. For where your treasure is, there will your heart be also. Let your loins be girded about, and *your* lights burning; And ye yourselves like unto men that wait for their lord, when he will return from the wedding; that when he cometh and knocketh, they may open unto him immediately. Blessed *are* those servants, whom the lord when he cometh shall find watching: verily I say unto you, that he shall gird himself, and make them to sit down to meat, and will come forth and serve them. And if he shall come in the second watch, or come in the third watch, and find *them* so, blessed are those servants. And this know, that if the goodman of the house had known what hour the thief would come, he would have watched, and not have suffered his house to be broken through. Be ye therefore ready also: for the Son of man cometh at an hour when ye think not.

Then Peter said unto him, Lord, speakest thou this parable unto us, or even to all?

And the Lord said, Who then is that faithful and wise steward, whom *his* lord shall make ruler over his household, to give *them their* portion of meat in due season? Blessed *is* that servant, whom his lord when he cometh shall find so doing. Of a truth I say unto you, that he will make him ruler over all that he hath. But and if that servant say in his heart, My lord delayeth his coming; and shall begin to beat the menservants and maidens, and to eat and drink, and to be drunken; The lord of that servant will come in a day when he looketh not for *him*, and at an hour when he is not aware, and will cut him in sunder, and will appoint him his portion with the unbelievers. And that servant, which knew his lord's will, and prepared not *himself*, neither did according to his will, shall be beaten with many *stripes*. But he that knew not, and did commit things worthy of stripes, shall be beaten with few *stripes*. For unto whomsoever much is given, of him shall be much required: and to whom men have committed much, of him they will ask the more.

The Parables of the Great Supper,
the Tower, and the Warring King
(From the Gospel of Luke)

And he put forth a parable to those which were bidden, when he marked how they chose out the chief rooms; saying unto them.

When thou art bidden of any *man* to a wedding, sit not down in the highest room; lest a more honourable man than thou be bidden of him; And he that bade thee and him come and say to thee, Give this man place; and thou begin with shame to take the lowest room. But when thou art bidden, go and sit down in the lowest room; that when he that bade thee cometh, he may say unto thee, Friend, go up higher: then shalt thou have worship in the presence of them that sit at meat with thee. For whosoever exalteth himself shall be abased; and he that humbleth himself shall be exalted.

Then said he also to him that bade him, When thou makest a dinner or a supper, call not thy friends, nor thy brethren, neither thy kinsmen, nor *thy* rich neighbours; lest they also bid thee again, and a recompence be made thee. But when thou makest a feast, call the poor, the maimed, the lame, the blind: And thou shalt be blessed; for they cannot recompense thee: for thou shalt be recompensed at the resurrection of the just.

And when one of them that sat at meat with him heard these things, he said unto him, Blessed is he that shall eat bread in the kingdom of God.

Then said he unto him, A certain man made a great supper, and bade many: And sent his servant at supper time to say to them that were bidden, Come; for all things are now ready. And they all with one *consent* began to make excuse. The first said unto him, I have bought a piece of ground, and I must needs go and see it: I pray thee have me excused. And another said, I have bought five yoke of oxen, and I go to prove them: I pray thee have me excused. And another said, I have married a wife, and therefore I cannot come. So that servant came, and shewed his lord these things. Then the master of the house being angry said to his servant, Go out quickly into the streets and lanes of the city, and bring in hither the poor, and the maimed, and the halt, and the blind. And the servant said, Lord, it is done as thou hast commanded, and yet there is room. And the lord said unto the servant, Go out into the highways and hedges, and compel *them* to come in, that my house may be filled. For I say unto you, That none of those men which were bidden shall taste of my supper.

And there went great multitudes with him: and he turned, and said unto them, If any *man* come to me, and hate not his father, and mother, and wife, and children, and brethren, and sisters, yea, and his own life also, he cannot be my disciple. And whosoever doth not bear his cross, and come after me, cannot be my disciple. For which of you, intending to build a tower, sitteth not down first, and counteth the cost, whether he have *sufficient* to finish *it?* Lest haply, after he hath laid the foundation, and is not able to finish *it,* all that behold *it* begin to mock him, Saying, This man began to build, and was not able to finish. Or what king, going to make war against another king, sitteth not down first, and consulteth whether he be able with ten thousand to meet him that cometh against him with twenty thousand? Or else, while the other is yet a great way off, he sendeth an ambassage, and desireth conditions of peace. So likewise, whosoever he be of you that forsaketh not all that he hath, he cannot be my disciple.

Salt *is* good: but if the salt have lost his savour, wherewith shall it be seasoned? It is neither fit for the land, nor yet for the dunghill; *but* men cast it out. He that hath ears to hear, let him hear.

The Parable of the Prodigal Son
(From the Gospel of Luke)

And he spake this parable unto them, saying, What man of you, having an hundred sheep, if he lose one of them, doth not leave the ninety and nine in the wilderness, and go after that which is lost, until he find it? And when he hath found *it,* he layeth *it* on his shoulders, rejoicing. And when he cometh home, he calleth together *his* friends and neighbours, saying unto them, Rejoice with me; for I have found my sheep which was lost. I say unto you, that likewise joy shall be in heaven over one sinner that repenteth, more than over ninety and nine just persons, which need no repentance.

Either what woman having ten pieces of silver, if she lose one piece, doth not light a candle, and sweep the house, and seek diligently till she find *it?* And when she hath found *it,* she calleth *her* friends and *her* neighbours together, saying, Rejoice with me; for I have found the piece which I had lost. Likewise, I say unto you, there is joy in the presence of the angels of God over one sinner that repenteth.

And he said, A certain man had two sons: And the younger of them said to *his* father, Father, give me the portion of goods that falleth *to me*. And he divided unto them *his* living. And not many days after the younger son gathered all together, and took his journey into a far country, and there wasted his substance with riotous living. And when he had spent all, there arose a mighty famine in that land; and he began to be in want. And he went and joined himself to a citizen of that country; and he sent him into his fields to feed swine. And he would fain have filled his belly with the husks that the swine did eat: and no man gave unto him. And when he came to himself, he said, How many hired servants of my father's have bread enough and to spare, and I perish with hunger! I will arise and go to my father, and will say unto him, Father, I have sinned against heaven, and before thee, And am no more worthy to be called thy son: make me as one of thy hired servants. And he arose, and came to his father. But when he was yet a great way off, his father saw him, and had compassion and ran, and fell on his neck, and kissed him. And the son said unto him, Father, I have sinned against heaven, and in thy sight, and am no more worthy to be called thy son. But the father said to his servants, Bring forth the best robe, and put *it* on him; and put a ring on his hand, and shoes on *his* feet: And bring hither the fatted calf, and kill *it;* and let us eat, and be merry: For this my son was dead, and is alive again; he was lost, and is found. And they began to be merry.

Now his elder son was in the field: and as he came and drew nigh to the house, he heard musick and dancing. And he called one of the servants, and asked what these things meant. And he said unto him, Thy brother is come; and thy father hath killed the fatted calf, because he hath received him safe and sound. And he was angry, and would not go in: therefore came his father out, and intreated him. And he answering said to *his* father, Lo, these many years do I serve thee, neither transgressed I at any time thy commandment: and yet thou never gavest me a kid, that I might make merry with my friends: But as soon as this thy son was come, which hath devoured thy living with harlots, thou hast killed for him the fatted calf. And he said unto him, Son, thou art ever with me, and all that I have is thine. It was meet that we should make merry, and be glad: for this thy brother was dead, and is alive again; and was lost, and is found.

The Parable of the Unjust Steward
(From the Gospel of Luke)

And he said also unto his disciples, There was a certain rich man, which had a steward; and the same was accused unto him that he had wasted his goods. And he called him, and said unto him, How is it that I hear this of thee? give an account of thy stewardship; for thou mayest be no longer steward. Then the steward said within himself, What shall I do? for my lord taketh away from me the stewardship: I cannot dig; to beg I am ashamed. I am resolved what to do, that, when I am put out of the stewardship, they may receive me into their houses. So he called every one of his lord's debtors *unto him,* and said unto the first, How much owest thou unto my lord? And he said, An hundred measures of oil. And he said unto him, Take thy bill, and sit down quickly, and write fifty. Then said he to another, And how much owest thou? And he said, An hundred measures of wheat. And he said unto him, Take thy bill, and write fourscore. And the lord commended the unjust steward, because he had done wisely: for the children of this world are in their generation wiser than the children of light. And I say unto you, Make to yourselves friends of the mammon of unrighteousness; that, when ye fail, they may receive you into everlasting habitations. He that is faithful in that which is least is faithful also in much: and he that is unjust in the least is unjust also in much. If therefore ye have not been faithful in the unrighteous mammon, who will commit to your trust the true *riches?* And if ye have not been faithful in that which is another man's, who shall give you that which is your own?

No servant can serve two masters: for either he will hate the one, and love the other; or else he will hold to the one, and despise the other. Ye cannot serve God and mammon.

The Parable of the Rich Man and Lazarus
(From the Gospel of Luke)

There was a certain rich man, which was clothed in purple and fine linen, and fared sumptuously every day: And there was a certain beggar named Lazarus, which was laid at his gate full of sores, And desiring to be fed with the crumbs which fell from the rich man's table: moreover the dogs came and licked his sores. And it came to pass, that the beggar died, and was carried by the angels into Abraham's bosom: the rich man also died, and was buried; And in hell he lift up his eyes, being in torments, and seeth Abraham afar off, and Lazarus in his bosom. And he cried and said, Father Abraham, have mercy on me, and send Lazarus, that he may dip the tip of his finger in water, and cool my tongue; for I am tormented in this flame. But Abraham said, Son, remember that thou in thy lifetime receivedst thy good things, and likewise Lazarus evil things: but now he is comforted, and thou art tormented. And beside all this, between us and you there is a great gulf fixed: so that they which would pass from hence to you cannot; neither can they pass to us, that *would come* from thence. Then he said, I pray thee therefore, father, that thou wouldest send him to my father's house: For I have five brethren; that he may testify unto them, lest they also come into this place of torment. Abraham saith unto him, They have Moses and the prophets; let them hear them. And he said, Nay, father Abraham: but if one went unto them from the dead, they will repent. And he said unto him, If they hear not Moses and the prophets, neither will they be persuaded, though one rose from the dead.

The Parables of the Importunate Widow
and of the Pharisee and the Publican
(From the Gospel of Luke)

And he spake a parable unto them to this end, that men ought always to pray, and not to faint; Saying, There was in a city a judge, which feared not God, neither regarded man; And there was a widow in that city; and she came unto him, saying, Avenge me of mine adversary. And he would not for a while: but afterward he said within himself, Though I fear not God, nor regard man: Yet because this widow troubleth me, I will avenge her, lest by her continual coming she weary me. *And the Lord said,* Hear what the unjust judge saith. And shall not God avenge his own elect, which cry day and night unto him, though he bear long with them? I tell you that he will avenge them speedily. Nevertheless when the Son of man cometh, shall he find faith on the earth?

And he spake this parable unto certain which trusted in themselves that they were righteous, and despised others:

Two men went up into the temple to pray: the one a Pharisee, and the other a publican. The Pharisee stood and prayed thus with himself. God, I thank thee, that I am not as other men *are*, extortioners, unjust, adulterers, or even as this publican. I fast twice in the week, I give tithes of all that I possess. And the publican, standing afar off, would not lift up so much as *his* eyes unto heaven, but smote upon his breast, saying, God be merciful to me a sinner. I tell you, this man went down to his house justified *rather* than the other; for every one that exalteth himself shall be abased; and he that humbleth himself shall be exalted.

The Parable of the Pounds
(From the Gospel of Luke)

He said therefore, A certain nobleman went into a far country to receive for himself a kingdom, and to return. And he called his ten servants, and delivered them ten pounds, and said unto them, Occupy till I come. But his citizens hated him, and sent a message after him, saying, We will not have this *man* to reign over us. And it came to pass, that when he was returned, having received the kingdom, then he commanded these servants to be called unto him, to whom he had given the money, that he might know how much every man had gained by trading. Then came the first, saying, Lord, thy pound hath gained ten pounds. And he said unto him, Well, thou good servant: because thou hast been faithful in a very little, have thou authority over ten cities. And the second came, saying, Lord, thy pound hath gained five pounds. And he said likewise to him, Be thou also over five cities. And another came, saying, Lord, behold *here is* thy pound, which I have kept laid up in a napkin. For I feared thee, because thou art an austere man: thou takest up that thou layedst not down, and reapest that thou didst not sow. And he saith unto him, Out of thine own mouth will I judge thee, *thou* wicked servant. Thou knewest that I was an austere man, taking up that I laid not down, and reaping that I did not sow: Wherefore then gavest not thou my money into the bank, that at my coming I might have required mine own with usury? And he said unto them that stood by, Take from him the pound, and give *it* to him that hath ten pounds. (And they said unto him, Lord, he hath ten pounds.) For I say unto you, That unto every one which hath shall be given; and from him that hath not, even that he hath shall be taken away from him. But those mine enemies, which would not that I should reign over them, bring hither, and slay *them* before me.

The Bread of Life
(From the Gospel of John)

I am that bread of life. Your fathers did eat manna in the wilderness, and are dead. This is the bread which cometh down from heaven, that a man may eat thereof, and not die. I am the living bread which came down from heaven: if any man eat of this bread, he shall live for ever: and the bread that I will give is my flesh, which I will give for the life of the world.

The Jews therefore strove among themselves, saying, How can this man give us his flesh to eat?

Then Jesus said unto them, Verily, verily, I say unto you, Except ye eat the flesh of the Son of man, and drink his blood, ye have no life in you. Whoso eateth my flesh, and drinketh my blood, hath eternal life; and I will raise him up at the last day. For my flesh is meat indeed, and my blood is drink indeed. He that eateth my flesh, and drinketh my blood, dwelleth in me, and I in him. As the living Father hath sent me, and I live by the Father: so he that eateth me, even he shall live by me. This is that bread which came down from heaven: not as your fathers did eat manna, and are dead: he that eateth of this bread shall live for ever.

The Good Shepherd and the Sheep
(From the Gospel of John)

Verily, verily, I say unto you, He that entereth not by the door into the sheepfold, but climbeth up some other way, the same is a thief and a robber. But he that entereth in by the door is the shepherd of the sheep. To him the porter openeth; and the sheep hear his voice: and he calleth his own sheep by name, and leadeth them out. And when he putteth forth his own sheep, he goeth before them, and the sheep follow him: for they know his voice. And a stranger will they not follow, but will flee from him: for they know not the voice of strangers.

This parable spake Jesus unto them: but they understood not what things they were which he spake unto them.

Then said Jesus unto them again, Verily, verily, I say unto you, I am the door of the sheep. All that ever came before me are thieves and robbers: but the sheep did not hear them. I am the door: by me if any man enter in, he shall be saved, and shall go in and out, and find pasture. The thief cometh not, but for to steal, and to kill, and to destroy: I am come that they might have life, and that they might have *it* more abundantly. I am the good shepherd: the good shepherd giveth his life for the sheep. But he that is an hireling, and not the shepherd, whose own the sheep are not, seeth the wolf coming, and leaveth the sheep, and fleeth: and the wolf catcheth them, and scattereth the sheep. The hireling fleeth, because he is an hireling, and careth not for the sheep. I am the good shepherd, and know my *sheep*, and am known of mine. As the Father knoweth me, even so know I the Father: and I lay down my life for the sheep. And other sheep I have, which are not of this fold: them also I must bring, and they shall hear my voice; and there shall be one fold, *and* one shepherd. Therefore doth my Father love me, because I lay down my life, that I might take it again. No man taketh it from me, but I lay it down of myself. I have power to lay it down, and I have power to take it again. This commandment have I received of my Father.

The True Vine
(From the Gospel of John)

I am the true vine, and my Father is the husbandman. Every branch in me that beareth not fruit he taketh away: and every *branch* that beareth fruit, he purgeth it, that it may bring forth more fruit. Now ye are clean through the word which I have spoken unto you. Abide in me, and I in you. As the branch cannot bear fruit of itself, except it abide in the vine; no more can ye, except ye abide in me. I am the vine, ye *are* the branches: He that abideth in me, and I in him, the same bringeth forth much fruit: for without me ye can do nothing. If a man abide not in me, he is cast forth as a branch, and is withered; and men gather them, and cast *them* into the fire, and they are burned. If ye abide in me, and my words abide in you, ye shall ask what ye will, and it shall be done unto you. Herein is my Father glorified, that ye bear much fruit; so shall ye be my disciples. As the Father hath loved me, so have I loved you: continue ye in my love. If ye keep my commandments, ye shall abide in my love; even as I have kept my Father's commandments, and abide in his love.

These things have I spoken unto you, that my joy might remain in you, and *that* your joy might be full. This is my commandment, That ye love one another, as I have loved you. Greater love hath no man than this, that a man lay down his life for his friends.

Thy Word Is Truth
(From the Gospel of John)

These words spake Jesus, and lifted up his eyes to heaven, and said, Father, the hour is come; glorify thy Son, that thy Son also may glorify thee: As thou hast given him power over all flesh, that he should give eternal life to as many as thou hast given him. And this is life eternal, that they might know thee the only true God, and Jesus Christ, whom thou hast sent. I have glorified thee on the earth: I have finished the work which thou gavest me to do. And now, O Father, glorify thou me with thine own self with the glory which I had with thee before the world was. I have manifested thy name unto the men which thou gavest me out of the world: thine they were, and thou gavest them me; and they have kept thy word. Now they have known that all things whatsoever thou hast given me are of thee. For I have given unto them the words which thou gavest me; and they have received *them*, and have known surely that I came out from thee, and they have believed that thou didst send me. I pray for them: I pray not for the world, but for them which thou hast given me;

for they are thine. And all mine are thine, and thine are mine; and I am glorified in them. And now I am no more in the world, but these are in the world, and I come to thee. Holy Father, keep through thine own name those whom thou hast given me, that they may be one, as we *are*. While I was with them in the world, I kept them in thy name: those that thou gavest me I have kept, and none of them is lost, but the son of perdition; that the scripture might be fulfilled. And now come I to thee; and these things I speak in the world, that they might have my joy fulfilled in themselves. I have given them thy word; and the world hath hated them, because they are not of the world, even as I am not of the world. I pray not that thou shouldest take them out of the world, but that thou shouldest keep them from the evil. They are not of the world, even as I am not of the world. Sanctify them through thy truth: thy word is truth. As thou hast sent me into the world, even so have I also sent them into the world. And for their sakes I sanctify myself, that they also might be sanctified through the truth. Neither pray I for these alone, but for them also which shall believe on me through their word; That they all may be one; as thou, Father, *art* in me, and I in thee, that they also may be one in us: that the world may believe that thou hast sent me. And the glory which thou gavest me I have given them;

that they may be one, even as we are one: I in them, and thou in me, that they may be made perfect in one; and that the world may know that thou hast sent me, and hast loved them, as thou hast loved me. Father, I will that they also, whom thou hast given me, be with me where I am; that they may behold my glory, which thou hast given me: for thou lovedst me before the foundation of the world. O righteous Father, the world hath not known thee: but I have known thee, and these have known that thou hast sent me. And I have declared unto them thy name, and will declare *it:* that the love wherewith thou hast loved me may be in them, and I in them.